VALENTINO FINDS A HOME

BY ANDY WHITESIDE

**ILLUSTRATED BY
CATHERINE HNATOV**

**Star Bright Books
Massachusetts**

*I would like to dedicate this book to my children
Samuel, Haydn, Elliot, Owen and Madeline. But
not forgetting a certain furry pig, Valentino, without
whom this book would not have been possible.
Whoop Whoop!!* —A.W.

Published in the United States of America by Star Bright Books, Inc.

The name Star Bright Books and the Star Bright Books logo are registered trademarks of Star Bright Books, Inc. Please visit www.starbrightbooks.com. For bulk orders, contact: orders@starbrightbooks.com, or call customer service at: (718) 784-9112.

Hardback ISBN-13: 978-1-59572-284-3
Paperback ISBN-13: 978-1-59572-286-7

Star Bright Books / MA / 00101120
Printed in China (WKT) 10 9 8 7 6 5 4 3 2 1

Library of Congress Cataloging-in-Publication Data

Whiteside, Andy.
Valentino finds a home / by Andy Whiteside ; illustrated by Catherine Hnatov.
    p. cm.
  Summary: Valentino the guinea pig runs away from Bolivia to find a safe home where people do not eat guinea pigs and do not mistake them for rats.
  ISBN-13: 978-1-59572-284-3 (hardcover)
  ISBN-10: 1-59572-284-X (hardcover)
  ISBN-13: 978-1-59572-286-7 (pbk.)
  ISBN-10: 1-59572-286-6 (pbk.)
  1. Guinea pigs--Juvenile fiction. 2. Pets--Juvenile fiction. [1. Stories in rhyme. 2. Guinea pigs--Fiction. 3. Pets--Fiction.] I. Hnatov, Catherine, ill. II. Title.
  PZ8.3.W5883Val 2011
  813.6--dc22
                                        2011002306

Valentino photographs by Todd Morgan. Additional photographic details: shutterstock.

Valentino is a guinea pig, ruffled, brown, and white.
He was born in Bolivia in the middle of the night.
But life for guinea pigs in Bolivia is often very tough.
There, people eat them and Valentino had had enough.
So he made a decision, "It's just not safe to stay,
I know what I'll do. I will run away."

Today's Special

Baked
Guinea
Pig!

So he ate a lot of carrots, and joined a special gym.

He lifted weights,

went running,

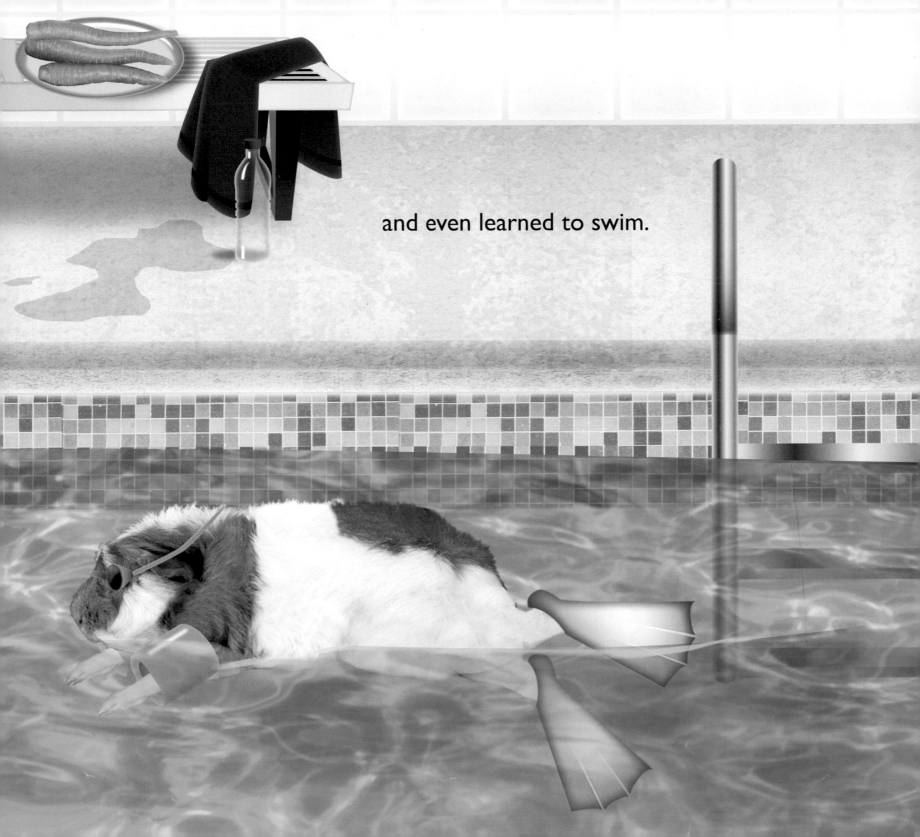

Once he was ready, he headed to the airport.
But security was high and a ticket couldn't be bought.
So, when no one was looking, he jumped into a case.
He buried deep beneath the clothes and no one saw his face.

Soon he fell asleep. Oh, how good he would feel!
To be just a happy guinea pig—no one's tasty meal.

The next thing he knew, he was woken from his dream.

The case was opened, and a lady let out a dreadful scream!

"A RAT! A RAT!" she loudly shouted, turning pale with fear.

"I'm not a rat," said Valentino, "now, let me make that clear."

"I'm a GUINEA PIG," he protested, "and I'm looking for a home . . ."

But the lady didn't listen, she was on the telephone.
She called her husband. "Come quickly! I've had a massive fright!
There's a rat inside our suitcase. I'm sure he was on our flight."

Her husband hurried home and found Valentino beneath his socks.
He picked him up gingerly and he put him in a box.

The man quickly took Valentino to the nearest pet store.
"Please take the rat inside this box, we don't want him anymore."

The storekeeper took the box and he had a look inside.
"I'm a GUINEA PIG, not a rat," Valentino cried.

But the storekeeper didn't hear him and he put him on the floor.

He was left there alone, and soon a man walked in the door.

"A dog, a fish, a cat? I have snakes, too.
I can get you anything, even a kangaroo."
"No, thank you," replied the man.
"None of them seem quite right.
She wants something small and furry, something that won't bite."

Then the man saw Valentino's box and took a look inside.

"What's this?" he asked the storekeeper.

"A return," was the reply.

"He's perfect," said the man. "It's exactly what I'll buy."

"How much is he, did you say?"

"He's free," said the storekeeper. "You can take him right away."

The man went home to Maddie. She was waiting by the door.
He carried the box inside and put it on the floor.
"Happy Birthday," he sang as she peeked inside the flap.
"I think you'll like it," said her dad, "it's a brown and white rat."

Maddie looked inside. She laughed and did a little jig.

"Dad, he's not a rat! He's a GUINEA PIG!"

Valentino jumped and danced and whistled loud with glee.

"At last! At last!" he cried, "Someone recognizes me!!"

"I love him! I love him!" Maddie screamed with sheer delight.
"I'll look after him, care for him, and I'll tuck him in at night."

Valentino was happy. No more would he have to roam,
He knew that he had found the perfect happy home.